THE ADVENTURER'S GUILD

THE COMPASS OF NEVER LOST

WRITTEN BY:
TIM GOEHLE

COVER ART:
MARK GOEHLE

ACKNOWLEDGEMENT

This is for every adventurer, swashbuckler, explorer, globetrotter, hero or heroine, pirate, daredevil, treasure-hunter, trailblazer, thrill-seeker and pathfinder who wishes to find excitement and adventure!

CHAPTER ONE

Wyll ran home from the bus stop and tossed his backpack onto the recliner in the living room. Then he dashed upstairs to his bedroom where he changed from his school uniform into a pair of camouflage cargo shorts and a Batman t-shirt. He headed back downstairs, sliding down the banister from the second floor and going straight towards the fridge where he grabbed a jug of chocolate milk and started drinking straight from it. In between gulps, he noticed a folded piece of paper lying on the floor by the door.

Someone must have slipped it through the mail drop, he thought. He put the jug down, then walked over to the front door and picked up the paper.

It was a message addressed to him. He stood in the hallway unfolding the paper and read the message.

Dear Walden Tiberius Forthchild (who also goes by the name Wyll),

My name is Thaddeus Thabletop the Third. I am a high adventurer and chairman of the new recruit welcoming committee. Let me be the first to welcome you to the Adventurer's Guild. We are a small but resourceful group of treasure hunters.

Our primary mission is to hunt down and recover rare, priceless and even sometimes magical artifacts. Once we successfully recover such artifacts we bring them to our headquarters. At which time we prepare them to be displayed for the entire world to appreciate, at the Museum of Rare and Wonderful Antiquites.

However, all things have a proper order and we must do first things first and leave second things for later. So please, stand up. Oh, you are already standing. Very good. Now hold this paper in your left hand and raise your right hand. Now recite after me...

I, Walden Tiberius Forthchild, do hereby agree that from this moment forward, I will seek and hunt any treasure or artifact that is assigned to me by the Adventurer's Guild. I will not allow any outside force to blockade, hinder, or stop me from accomplishing this task. Even if this means the loss of limb or life. So help me God!

"Loss of life?" Wyll said scrunching up his face. He continued to read.

...Of course there are exceptions and those can be found in the Treasure Hunter's Handbook, which I will personally hand to you. And now since you have been properly indoctrinated into the Adventurer's Guild and been transformed into a world class treasure hunter. I will be bringing you the first task. I will be knocking on your door shortly, please let me in.

Indubiously Yours,
Thaddeus Thabletop III
High Adventurer Recruiter

Wyll looked up from the paper at the front door but nothing happened. He was just turning to walk back into the kitchen when three loud knocks sounded on the front door. He couldn't believe his ears. Wyll reluctantly looked through the peephole and saw the strangest person he had ever laid eyes on.

The man was dressed in a brown tweed suit jacket with green patches on the elbows and brown cargo pants. Under the jacket the man wore an orange button-down shirt with a red and blue plaid bow tie. He had on an old khaki hat and his bright white hair was sticking out wildly from underneath it. Bushy white eyebrows almost hid a pair of shockingly gray eyes and his mustache looked a bit out of control.

"Walden," the old man called out, "can you please let me in? It's very hot out here and I'm afraid I didn't dress properly. I told you in the letter that I was coming, didn't I?"

He opened the door and stared wide-eyed at the old man, who didn't wait for an invitation and simply walked into the house. He took his coat off and hung it on the coat rack next to the door.

"My friends call me Wyll," he told him, not sure what else to say.

"Of course they do," he responded," and I'm Thaddeus. Not only will I be your recruiter but I've been assigned as your advisor and guide during your first few missions."

"Now hold on. I don't understand," Wyll said. "Why did you send me that letter?"

"Because it was addressed to you, of course."

"No, I mean why did you send it to me? I'm not a treasure hunter."

"Did you not find your sisters cat three times just last week? And a couple of weeks before that you recovered your best friend's baseball card collection."

"So? Those things aren't important."

"See? You're the perfect candidate. Here's your handbook and your first mission," Thaddeus said to him as he handed him a small dark blue leather-bound book and a letter sealed with a wax stamp. The stamp had the letters A & G overlapping within a shield. Wyll stared down at the book and the letter in his hands. Meanwhile, the old man cheerfully tromped into the kitchen and began eating some watermelons slices out of the fridge. Wyll looked up from the book, his mouth gaping open in confusion, just in time to see Thaddeus slip his coat back on and make his way out of the house.

"I do love watermelon so very much," he said, munching as he went.

The old man was gone before he knew it, so Wyll didn't really have time to ask any questions or refuse this crazy notion of him being a treasure hunter.

He looked closer at the cover and saw the words "Treasure Hunter's Handbook" inscribed on the bottom edge. When he looked up, the old man was at the street about to get into an old black car with a high round top. Thaddeus looked back at Wyll and tipped his hat. Then he climbed into car right before it sped away.

"*Wow!*" Wyll thought, "*that driver was in a hurry.*" He didn't know what to do, so he went to the den to read the letter.

CHAPTER TWO

Wyll sank into the large leather recliner in the den. He pulled back the lever on the side of the chair, extending the foot rest out. He peeled open the envelope and pulled out a shabby piece of parchment paper with the same style writing from the previous letter. He glanced back at the front door occasionally, expecting to hear Thaddeus knock on the door again. Then he read the letter. It gave him detailed instructions to follow the next morning.

Wyll,

Go downtown tomorrow to Ficklestein's Fine Parchments & Stationary. It sits on the corner of 5th Avenue and Treacher Street. Only four blocks from Main Street. Go to the back of the store and you will find an oversized green quill pen standing upright in an ink well. Push the quill towards the portrait of the tabby cat on the wall twice and pull it back towards you once, all while reciting the following phrase: I am here to hunt for treasure, through every trial and terrible weather. I will not stop until I have it.

Indubiously,

Thaddeus Thabletop 3rd

He slipped the letter into the back of the handbook, then began flipping through the handbook, just to see what was in it. Wyll went to the brief table of contents. The book was separated into four different chapters.

1. History of the Adventurer's Guild

2. Rules and Regulations for Treasure Hunters

3. Adventurer's Guild Tactics & Strategies

4. Maps & Known Treasures (Found & Unfound)

The first two chapters were very boring and there were a few pictures scattered throughout the history and rules. The last two sections were different; they were littered with maps, diagrams and pictures. . The pictures were particularly fascinating, showing everything from different treasures that had been found by the Adventurer's Guild, to others that were still missing. There were even pictures of some strange looking creatures. All of the drawings were sketched by hand. Even if this was all bogus, the book still was cool looking.

Wyll couldn't help himself and began reading Chapter three eventually becoming so engrossed that he lost track of time. The grandfather clock in the living room chimed loudly causing him to jump from the chair. His father and mother would be home in thirty minutes. He gathered all the stuff and took it to his bedroom. It was Friday night, and Friday night meant pizza night.

He just finished reading about the treasure hunter's rules in the handbook, when he heard his father coming into the house through the garage door. Shortly after, his father called him down for dinner. Except this time, the pizza he expected wasn't there. A large bowl of spaghetti and meatballs sat in the center of the table.

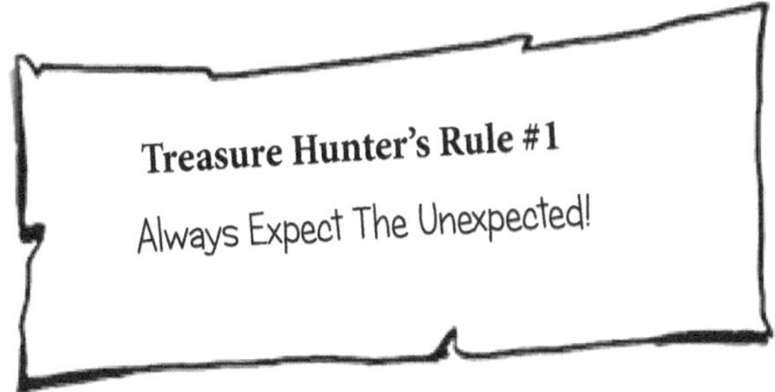

CHAPTER THREE

It was eight o'clock in the morning and Wyll was awake, which was something new for him on a Saturday. The sun was just starting to come over the neighbor's roof and light shined brightly into his window. He made up his mind last night. He was going to do what the strange old man said. It was the only way he would be able to get some answers.

He filled a blue backpack with the list of needed items found in the Treasure Hunter's Handbook. He grabbed a flashlight, a rope, a notebook with pencils and a pocket knife. Then he tossed in some fruit snacks and a granola bar just incase. He stepped quietly downstairs only to find his father at the breakfast bar eating some french toast and reading a magazine about investments.

"Where are you headed so early in the morning?" his father asked without taking his eyes from the magazine.

"Meeting a friend down at the skate park," Wyll told his father. "We want to get some practice in before the skater kids get there."

"Who are you going with?"

"Theodore," Wyll said, almost slipping and saying Thaddeus.

"Who?" his father asked, turning from the magazine and looking at his son.

"Ted, I meant," Wyll tried to recover. "It's short for Theodore."

"I know that, son. Do I know him?"

"He's the one with the green bike that made it to the quarter finals with me."

"The one with the jet black hair?"

"Yeah, that's him."

"Oh, okay," he said. "Well, have fun and be safe. When will you be home?"

"After lunch," Wyll said as he ran out the door into the garage. He grabbed his bike off the wall hooks and checked the air in his tires. He pushed the button and the garage door opened automatically. Wyll felt terrible lying to his father about where he was going, but there was no way that his dad would let him go otherwise.

Wyll had a blue Mongoose BMX. It was the most favorite thing he owned next to his PlayStation. He rode the bike everywhere; he would ride it to the mall just to meet his mother and sister who often drove there in the jeep to go shopping. On weekends, Wyll would compete in either BMX races or freestyle competitions.

It didn't take him long to make it downtown. He knew all of the short cuts, such as; cutting through Cornelius Park, which was named after the founding family of Beachville. He jumped off his bike as he approached the store and quickly chained it to the wrought iron gate around the tree in front of the store.

He must have gone by this place at least once a week on his way to the library or the ice cream shop. He couldn't remember if he had ever been inside with his mother, probably not if he couldn't remember. The door made a dinging sound when he opened it. A little old lady with a light pink hue to her hair sat behind the counter. She barely lifted her head when he came in, but she smiled at him pleasantly in greeting. There were three rows of stationary in the shop. *Nice stuff in here*, he thought as he headed to the back of the store.

Just as the letter said there was a four-foot-high table with an inkwell in the center of it. Sticking out from the ink was a large quill pen with an oversized green feather on top of it. And right behind the pen was the portrait of a tabby cat. The only thing different was that the painting was of a tabby cat sitting in a high-back maroon chair. He was wearing black rimmed reading glasses with a copy of Sherlock Holmes in his lap. It was a strange picture.

Wyll took the quill in his right hand and pushed it towards the wall twice and pulled it back while he recited the saying from the letter. He'd practiced it all morning until he had it right.

"I am here to hunt for treasure, through every trial and terrible weather. I will not stop until I have it," he recited as he moved the quill pen.

The wall behind the table pulled back away from him. It was hinged at the top, causing it to swing upwards towards the ceiling. The table was attached to the wall, so it disappeared up into the ceiling. As it pulled away, it revealed a long, straight staircase leading down.

The walls surrounding the stairs were made out of large gray stones and didn't fit into the decor of the stationary store. It reminded him of the dungeons in some of the games he played, all it needed was torches on the walls. At the bottom of the stairs was a purple oval door with a brass knob in the dead center of it. He went down the stairs, taking two at a time. When he reached the bottom, a small lens popped out of the door just above the door knob. Before he knew it, a blue beam scanned Wyll from head to toe and then the door clicked, swinging open.

CHAPTER FOUR

A large room with fifteen foot high ceilings was revealed behind the purple oval door. A bunch of whiteboards and corkboards were attached to the wall on the left side of the room. Memos, photos, and maps were pinned all over them. The right wall had a desk that ran half the length with three large computers on it. Wyll looked closer and saw they were just large screens with the drives built into the side of the monitors. A large brown wooden book shelf and fridge stood next to the desk. The wall straight across from the door had a strange looking door frame with no door in it. Within in the frame was just the wall.

In the dead center of the room there was a cement block three feet tall and three feet wide with brass edges. Wyll stood in front of the large stone block with brass plates on the corners, in the middle of the room.

On top of of the block was a twelve inch square speaker, with a blue metal rim, right in the center. He moved a little closer to get a better look. Within the rim there was a single camera lens at both the top and the bottom. Then one more to each the left and right side. Each lens was marked with a letter H, T, H, and S. As he got closer to the cube, the projectors turned on and a hologram of Thaddeus Thabletop's face was projected above the block from the four camera lenses. The speaker in the middle of the rim crackled to life.

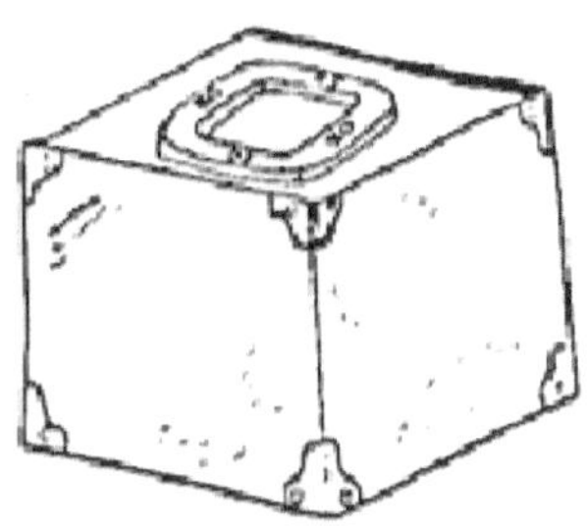

"It's good to see that you could make it, Wyll," Thaddeus said to him.

"It wasn't too hard," he responded.

"I am going to get right to the point. Over a thousand years ago there was a monk who traveled around the world. As he grew older he decided to settle down in the woods between Beachville and Valleytown. This artifact is very close to your home and that is why I've chosen this to be your first mission. You see, the travelling monk was a collector of rare and wonderful artifacts. The Adventurer's Guild has recovered the majority of his artifacts, but one has continued to elude us. And that's where you come into the situation."

"Me?" Wyll asked. "What am I looking for?"

"It is called the Compass of Never Lost."

"And it's somewhere in the woods between the two towns?"

"No," Thaddeus told him. "We're led to believe that the compass was discovered when Ryker Nickels purchased the old monk's land and cabin. Do you know who I speak off, Wyll?"

"Uh huh, isn't he the guy that ran the old mines in the mountains?"

"None other."

"I thought he died in a plane crash."

"He did," Thaddeus informed him, "but we believe that before he died he discovered what he had in his possession and then hid it in the mines for safe-keeping. We have looked everywhere else."

"A compass?"

"Not just any compass, the Compass of Never Lost," he told him. "When you think of the place you want to go while holding it in your hand and ask it to, 'lead the way to that which I seek,' it'll shine a white light in the direction that you should go."

"Cool! How does it do that?"

"There are many wonderful things in the world, Wyll, but sadly we don't know how most of these things work."

"Like magic?"

"Just like magic."

Thabletop's face vanished and was replaced with the image of a gold-colored compass. It wasn't your ordinary compass. On it's face there wasn't any hands to show which way you were going. In the middle, behind a glass face, there was an eye carved into the face of compass. The edge resembled the woven design of a rope and on the back of the compass, a saying was etched into it.

Eye will show you the way...

The image of the compass continued to turn and flip over, showing Wyll all angles of it. After a few minutes, Thabletop's face returned and the compass vanished.

"I have taken the liberty of bringing in some assistance for your first mission. We've notified another treasure hunter living right here in Beachville."

"You did?"

"Do you know Annora Easton?"

"Do I ever!" Wyll almost shouted. "She's the most beautiful girl in school. And I also heard she surfs and is an awesome freestyle BMX biker."

"Wonderful! You will find her standing right behind you," Thaddeus informed him, "Miss Easton, Meet Wyll."

Wyll slapped his hands to his face, "aw, man," he complained, muffling the words. He turned, looking up to see Annora standing by the bottom of the staircase just looking at him with a silly smirk on her face. She was two years older than Wyll and was in her last year at their middle school. Her long, curly brown hair was tied back in a ponytail under a baseball hat with an image of the Silver Surfer on the front of it. She had brown eyes and looked like she spent just the right amount of time at the beach to get a perfect tan.

"How long have you been there?" he asked her.

"Don't worry, lover boy," she responded, walking into the room. "I'm just here to do a job. But maybe I can teach you to surf afterwards."

He just looked at the ceiling and shook his head, "You know for a hologram of a head," he said, turning around, "you're not very helpful. You could have warned me about her sooner."

"It doesn't matter," Thaddeus told him.

"Where do we start?" Annora asked, coming along side Wyll.

The hologram machine projected an image across the room onto one of the whiteboards. It was a painting of Mr. Nickels as an older man; three young children surrounded him. Wyll walked over to get a closer look.

"What's so important about this painting?" he asked the hologram.

"It's a painting of Nickels with his grandchildren, but on the back we believe that there's a map of the mines.

If you could get into the house somehow and get a look at the back of the painting, then you may be able to figure out where in the mines it was hidden."

"How do we get into the house to see the map?"

"You'll have to figure that out," Thaddeus stated, "that's why you're Treasure Hunters! Just be careful out there and follow the rules in your handbook. Everything else will fall into place."

"We need to concentrate on finding a way for them to let us into the Nickels mansion," Annora told Wyll. "I don't want to go to jail for breaking and entering. Homecoming is next week and I got invited. I don't want to miss it." As if on cue, the hologram of Thaddeus Thabletop flickered out of existence.

She walked over to the maps of town and started mapping out a route from the store to the Nickels mansion. Then connected that to the mines with an additional line.

Wyll went over to the computers and started to scour the internet looking for something they could use.

After an eternity of searching, he found something. "Jackpot," he called out, waving Annora over to show her. It was an article featuring Paige Nickels, the youngest daughter and owner of the estate. She was in the library showing the newspaper a collection of rare model trains. Hanging on the wall behind the daughter was the painting that they needed to get their hands on.

"So?" she said.

"So? If we go to the house and tell her we're doing a report for school on Mr. Nickels and his train collection, she might just let us into the room where the trains and the painting is."

"It might work," she said, changing her tune.

"It will work," he assured her.

They gathered all of their stuff and ran upstairs to the bikes. Wyll already liked this treasure hunting thing and it was just the first day. Though he had to admit that it could have something to do with the fact that he was riding beside Annora Easton

Maybe.

CHAPTER FIVE

Wyll and Annora rode their bikes through the center of town heading towards the Nickel's family estate. It was located on the far side of town in the more affluent neighborhood of Green Lake. The estate took up the entire length of Cherry Blossom Trail. They used the bike ride to conjure up a good story, so they could get into the library and close to the painting. It wasn't long before they were surrounded by cherry blossom trees. It was fall, so there weren't any blooms on the trees yet. The sprawling mansion sat at the end of the street on a cul-de-sac.

The house itself was a beautiful craftsman-style home, but to Wyll it looked like it was the size of a castle. It was made of elegant, dark colored woods and large gray river stones. A porch wrapped around the entire front and both sides.

The front entryway had two huge, intricately carved wooden statues of grizzly bears. Their arms were stretched out above their heads, supporting a small balcony on the second floor. They looked very intimidating. Wyll imagined them coming to life and attacking any intruders. Annora pushed him forward, then slid in behind him. He knocked on the door using the huge wooden knocker attached in the center of the door. It was a large wooden ring held by the mouth of another bear. The doors were large and curved at the top.

Shortly after knocking, the door swung open to reveal a seven-foot-tall butler. He had a sloping forehead, a long face, and Cro-Magnon type arms to match. He looked down his nose at both of them, and they took an unconscious step back from the freakishly big man.

"May I help you?" the butler asked in a very deep monotone voice.

"Is, uhm, Miss Nickels here?" Wyll asked.

"Indeed, she is," he said to them, raising his left eyebrow. "Who may I say is requesting her presence?"

His throat suddenly became dry and scratchy. "My name's Wyll and this is Annora," he finally managed to say.

"We've got a research report we're doing for school on Mr. Nickels and we still need more information," Annora added, stepping out from behind Wyll.

"Yeah," Wyll added, "it's about his big collection of model trains."

"I see. Please wait right here," the butler commanded, then he shut the door. They could hear his large feet thudding against the stone floors as he walked off to retrieve Miss Nickels. Wyll hoped that she would be a little more welcoming and warmer than the butler. He was actually a bit scary.

A short time later the front door swung open again and a petite old lady with silver blue hair wearing an emerald green dress stood in the doorway. The butler remained by her side, towering over them all. His hands were enormous and Wyll couldn't help imaging that he could probably crush a human skull. He decided to keep out of reach of the butler.

"How may I help you kids?" Miss Nickels asked in the sweetest and kindest voice the kids had ever heard.

"We have a school report," Annora responded in her own sweet voice, "on famous people in our town and we decided to do our report on Mr. Nickels. Unfortunately, there was just too much to write about so after reading an article in the Beachville Tribune, we narrowed it down to his impressive train collection."

"Oh, you'll be in for such a treat," she told them, "Ryker was an avid train collector and his collection is extremely beautiful."

"Do you think we could see the trains?" Wyll asked.

"I don't see any harm in it. William, my butler, can take you to the library. The most important pieces are on display there. I wish I could join you but I have an urgent meeting in town."

Miss Nickels smiled at the children and left them alone with the foreboding butler. They could hear her saying something about sweet children as she walked across the large foyer and through a door leading into the kitchen. The butler didn't say a word, he simply turned and started walking away. The kids followed behind, trying to keep up with the pace of his long legs. The front door shut behind them and made a loud clicking sound that echoed throughout the house as it closed.

William led them straight to a room that could have resembled the Library of Congress, stretching his hands out to urge them in.

The Nickels' library was humongous, on the walls was nothing but bookshelves and beautiful paintings. It consisted of two floors, and the second floor had a lot more bookshelves wrapping around the room. There weren't as many paintings up there but a few were on display between the shelves. The train collection was displayed on stands throughout the room and a large train layout dominated the center of the bottom floor. A tall metal ladder on wheels was attached to a railing that ran along the perimeter of the room, giving access to both levels.

Unfortunately, they didn't see the painting that they were looking for hanging on the walls. However, Miss Nickels was correct about her brother's train collection, there were plenty of high quality and beautiful trains everywhere. After they entered room, William shut the door behind them without saying a single word. Then they heard the door click.

"I think he just locked us in here," Wyll said.

"He did," Annora told him, "but we need to find that painting and then we'll figure a way out of here."

They split up to look for it, with Annora looking around at the paintings on the bottom floor while Wyll climbed up to the second floor. The painting could be hidden anywhere. Wyll wasn't having any luck until he found a small alcove in the back corner of the second floor. There were a bunch of older paintings being stored in it; altogether there were about fifteen. He quickly searched through them and found the one they were looking for near the back of the stack.

"I got it!" he called down to Annora.

"Good," she said, quickly climbing the ladder to join him on the second floor.

"Here we are," he said, showing her the painting.

"Awesome! And just in time, too. I think we need to get going."

"Why?"

"Our friend gigantor, the butler, just met someone out in the driveway. I don't know what they were talking about but he was pointing towards the library and the other man looked very sinister."

"Sinister?"

"Yeah, everything on him was black except his bright white skin. A black coat and pants, shoes, hair, mustache, and all that topped off with a black bowler hat. Even the cane he was holding was black with a silver handle."

"Well then let's get out of here! What are we going to do with the map?" Wyll asked.

"Open the frame and pull the map out of the back."

She took the frame from Wyll then turned it over, pulling out the tacks, which held the back in place. They could hear the front door shutting and the footsteps of the men coming down the hall towards the library.

After she got the back wooden panel off the frame, an old piece of parchment fell to the floor. Wyll quickly grabbed it from the floor and glanced at it to make sure it was a map. Then he folded it up and tucked it into one of his cargo pockets. The two of them slid the painting back into place behind the other ones in the alcove.

"What now?"

"Out the window," Annora said, pointing to the window on the opposite side of the second floor.

"Are you sure?" he asked her. "We're pretty high up."

"Of course, I'm sure," she told him. "Come on, let's go."

Annora ran over to the window with Wyll close behind her. She was sliding it open when they heard the sound of the door being unlocked. As the door was opening she climbed out the window and jumped without so much as a pause.

Wyll stuck his head out the window to see Annora already running across the estate's well-maintained grounds. He was extremely nervous but quickly climbed out the window when he heard the man in the bowler hat yell across the library, "Hey, you, kid!"

Wyll took a deep breath and then jumped out the window. The unmovable ground came quicker then he thought it would and it was as if a jolt of lightning shot through his body. He crumpled to the ground instead of rolling with the landing like he was supposed to.

It took him a few seconds longer but Wyll was soon on his feet and running to his bike. Annora was holding it up for him. By the time the man in black stuck his head out the second floor window, the kids were pedaling down Cherry Blossom Lane.

CHAPTER SIX

Wyll and Annora sat in the far booth just outside the entrance to the kitchen in *Sandy's Cafe & Bistro*, a small cafe that served breakfast and lunch only, right in the middle of downtown Beachville. The owner, Sandra Mulligan, was a young woman with shoulder length strawberry blond hair and light blue eyes. According to Annora, she was a supporter for the Adventurer's Guild and provided a safe haven for visiting members. Her nephew, Phillip, was a treasure hunter from a town up in the north.

Sandy placed an egg salad sandwich on rye bread in front of Wyll and gave Annora her world famous bacon, lettuce, and tomato panini with fries. The cafe had won multiple awards for the sandwiches they serve; the actual plaques and medals hung on the wall behind the counter.

The rest of the wall was covered by pictures of people that had visited the cafe. Annora scrunched her face while Wyll stuffed the egg salad sandwich into his mouth.

"I can't believe you really eat that stuff," she said to him. "I thought only my grandmother ate that."

"Whatever," he told her with a shrug of his shoulders. "I think it's delicious."

She just shook her head and took a bite from her sandwich. Wyll told a few jokes and they both laughed together. They talked about their bikes and some new freestyle tricks. She promised to teach him to surf someday. Living in a town called Beachville, he felt that knowing how to surf was important and she agreed. When they were finished with their sandwiches, he pulled the map out and spread it across the table.

"It looks like a map of the mines. It's got an entrance here, see?" Annora pointed out.

"There's some writing on it," he told her. "I think they're clues of some sort."

Annora leaned in a little closer to read the writing on the bottom of the map. It looked like someone wrote it in after the fact. *The rusty blue lantern is the key; beneath its guiding light, the treasure you'll see...*

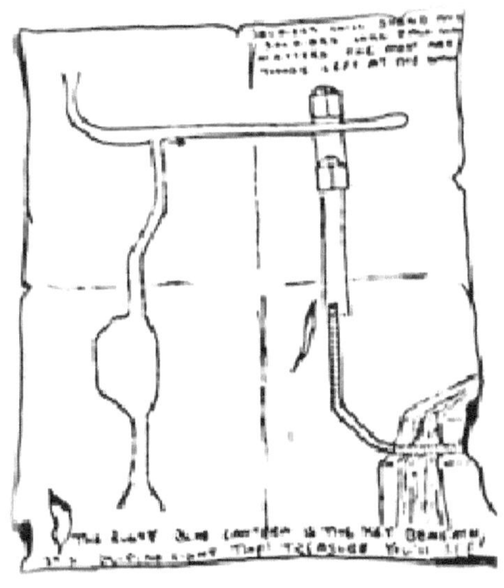

"What do you think it means?" he asked.

"I don't know."

"Look here," he said, pointing to a drawing on the map that looked like an elevator. It also had some writing next to it. *Soldiers will rise and soldiers will fall; what matters the most are those left at the wall.*

"It doesn't make sense to me," he added.

"It'll probably all make more sense when we get to the mines," she told him.

Annora got up from the table with her lemonade. She also grabbed Wyll's empty glass of root beer and headed to the counter for refills. A large gray sedan with very dark tinted windows was parked across the street from the cafe. Sandy was looking out the front window at the car when Annora startled her and she jumped a bit.

"What's wrong?" Annora asked her as she put the glasses down on the counter.

"The Black Wolf," she told the young girl, nodding towards the car. "I saw him lurking around town earlier this morning. You can bet that he's here for the compass."

"Is he dangerous?"

"He's a villain," she warned her, "and the worst kind."

"He wouldn't happen to wear all black and a bowler hat?"

"Yes, that would be him. Why?"

"We saw him today at the Nickel's estate."

"Hmm," Sandy contemplated the news. "I think you should leave here through the back. Leave the Wolf wondering where you went."

"What about our bikes?"

"Leave the bikes. It'll complete the ruse. I'll call someone to come get you. In the meantime, just head back to your table."

Annora nodded in agreement and took the refilled drinks back to the table with Wyll. She slid back into her seat and smiled at Wyll. He could tell there was something wrong.

"What is it?"

"The guy we saw at the mansion is following us," she told him.

"What!" Wyll said, almost jumping out of his seat. "How do you know?"

"Sit down," Annora tried to whisper but it came out a little louder than she wished and the other people in the cafe turned to look at them. Wyll realized that he was making a scene and slid back out of view of the other patrons.

"He's in a car outside the cafe and is obviously after us."

"What's the plan?"

"We're going out the back and Sandy is going to get us a ride to the mines."

After fifteen minutes or so, Sandy walked over and placed a large piece of chocolate cake between the two kids. She nodded her head towards the back door. "Your ride is here," she told them. Annora excused herself from the table and Sandy made her way back up to the front of the café, standing between the kids and the Black Wolf, trying to block them from view.

Annora disappeared down the hallway and out the rear door into the back parking lot.

Wyll's eyes almost popped out of his head looking at the cake. As soon as Annora got up from the table he stabbed his fork into the cake and began shoveling it into his mouth. He would rather have a cold glass of milk with it, but the root beer would just have to do.

After devouring the cake, he made his way to the back parking lot where he saw a forest green FJ Cruiser sitting with its engine idling. The top of the vehicle was bright white and the Cruiser looked like it was aching to go off-roading. Annora was standing next to it with the passenger door open, waiting for Wyll to climb into the back seat. In the driver's seat was a tall man with tan skin, wavy dirty blond hair, and hazel eyes. He was wearing a light blue shirt, tan board shorts, and flip-flops. It was obvious that Sandy had pulled him away from the local beach.

Wyll climbed in and noticed the crest for the Adventurer's Guild on his key chain. Annora flipped the seat back and climbed in the front. Then the man put the Cruiser into drive and took off out of the parking lot.

"So what's your name, little dude?" the man asked, looking through the rear view mirror at Wyll.

"Wyll," he answered.

"Well, my name's Kipling Kobblestone and Sandy said that you guys needed a lift to avoid the Black Wolf. Anything I can do to stick it to the Wolf makes me happy." Both of the kids laughed at that statement along with Kipling. "So where are we heading?"

"We need to get to the Nickels mines," Wyll said

"You want Stryker's Peak," Kipling said.

He turned down Appleton Boulevard and headed out of town towards the mountain that was home to the mines.

Hopefully the Black Wolf had no clue...

CHAPTER SEVEN

Kipling pulled off onto a small embankment halfway up the mountainside of Stryker's Peak. The kids climbed out of the Cruiser. They had a mile to hike through the woods before reaching the entrance of the abandoned mines. Since the mining operations had stopped many years ago the road was now completely overgrown. It had just stopped raining and the trees were glistening with water. A cold wind was blowing in from the north and with it came a low-lying mist creeping around the bushes. Wyll thought it was a rather fitting atmosphere for their mission.

"Let's get moving," Annora said, "before the Wolf figures out that we're not in the cafe anymore."

"You guys be safe, okay?" Kipling called out to them from the inside of the Cruiser. "If I know the Wolf, he probably knows that you're gone already."

"Do you think he'll still come after us?" Wyll asked Kipling.

"If he knows where you're heading, then he'll definitely come after you."

"C'mon," Annora called back to Wyll, already disappearing into the edge of the forest.

"You better get a move on, dude. She'll leave you behind," Kipling told him.

"Thanks for the ride," Wyll said as he shut the door, then he tightened the straps on his back pack and ran after Annora.

The two of them moved as quickly as they could; the ground was damp from the rain and covered with slippery wet leaves. They didn't want to be slowed down by a fall. Their clothes were already becoming damp from the wet bushes and with the cold breeze they felt a chill run through them. Annora kept glancing behind to make sure that nobody was following them and that the trail remained empty.

They hiked up a hill to a small clearing that formed a pleasant glade. The entrance to mines sat across the glade. The mouth of the mine was over fifteen feet tall and just as wide. Large wide wooden boards crisscrossed the entrance, keeping out would-be trespassers. Signs were posted on the boards and next to the entrance, warning people to stay away. They walked over to the entrance and Wyll peered in between the boards trying to figure out how to get in.

He grabbed onto the edge of a board and pulled as hard as he could digging his feet into the ground. He pulled so hard his face felt like it was about to explode. He collapsed to the ground all red faced and panting. Annora stepped around him with a large branch and slid it in a small opening between two of the boards. Using the branch created a lever effect, allowing her to pop off a board with ease.

"Good thing I loosened that up, "Wyll said, dusting himself off hastily, "or we may never have gotten in there." He slid his back pack through the opening first, then crawled in behind it.

"Of course," she said as she followed him into the mines. Wyll tried to pretend he didn't see her smirking.

The entrance was very dark inside, as the boards did a great job keeping the sunlight from creeping into the cave. Wyll pulled his flashlight out of his back pack but it wouldn't turn on.

He smacked the handle with his palm a couple of times, but the batteries must have been dead.

"Really?" Annora sighed. "You didn't check your batteries before putting that in your bag?"

"I did," he promised her. "It worked just fine when I pulled it off the dresser."

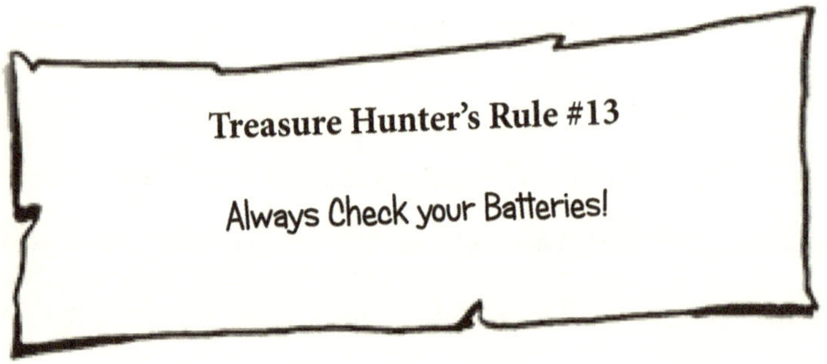

"Maybe it was turned on in your backpack and the battery drained. Either way, it doesn't matter, we need to keep moving." She pulled out a small Maglite from her pocket. It may have been a small flashlight but when she turned it on the cave illuminated like the sun was in the mine.

They walked further into the mine guided by Annora's flashlight. They came to a very large room just thirty or forty yards from the entrance. It was a huge open room about sixty feet high. An old two-story building on stilts sat off to the left side of the space. The stairs leading up to the first floor of the building were broken and useless. Luckily there was another ladder that led to a platform straight across from the building. A wooden suspension bridge connected the platform to the building. It was high enough for trucks to drive underneath it while they were loaded with supplies. Unfortunately the stairs leading to the platform didn't look that safe either, but at least they were still intact.

"This is the Cathedral Room," Annora told him.

"How do you know that?" he asked her.

"I did some research on my phone while Kipling drove us here. The stalactites resemble flying buttresses from gothic cathedrals, hence the name Cathedral Room."

"Stalactites?"

"Yeah," she said, pointing at the ceiling. "The pointed rocks hanging from the ceiling of the mines are called stalactites and the ones growing up from the ground are called stalagmites."

"Cool," Wyll said as he slowly walked up the stairs leading to the platform. He tried to stay as close as possible to the edge of the stairs; it seemed the safest path. The wooden stairs creaked with each step and he was convinced only a prayer kept him from tumbling to the ground. Annora stayed close behind him so that the light helped them both. When they got to the top, the platform seemed to sway underneath their feet.

"Be careful," Wyll said. "This whole place seems like it could collapse at any moment."

"Let's just hurry up and get over to the building," she said, gently nudging him forward. "I just hope the lantern is in there."

"Lantern?"

"The old rusty blue one," she reminded him. "The one the map told us about."

"Oh, yeah!"

He carefully walked across the old wooden bridge, thinking the entire time that it was going to fall apart under his feet at any moment. The bridge brought them straight to the second floor. The building was made of wood paneling and it looked like the second floor had a room added on after it was built. The second floor was bigger than the first floor and that made it look odd. The only two windows on the front of the building were so filthy he couldn't see through them. At first Wyll had trouble opening the door but after a swift kick with the bottom of his foot the door swung open and even broke off the top hinge.

It stayed open just hanging crookedly on a single hinge. He looked back at Annora and shrugged his shoulders; she just shook her head. Wyll grabbed the light from her and went inside the building.

CHAPTER EIGHT

The Wolf slammed his fist into the steering wheel, causing the car to jerk to the right a little. He yelled into the microphone of his hands-free phone. He just shook his head in frustration. The notorious and dangerous Black Wolf, duped by two kids. He wouldn't let that happen again.

On the other end of the phone conversation was, Mrs. Josephine, the technical wizard and field agent liaison for the greedy worldwide organization of B&P International. It was named after two villains that started it back in the early 1940s.

To the public, it was a global investment and entertainment corporation, but those were just legitimate fronts for the company. The true purpose of the organization, the one that lurked in the shadows, was a criminal empire whose only goal was wealth and power.

They had spread their corrupt and dirty philosophies throughout the world, earning them the title of The Black Plague. They destroyed anything that got in their way.

"I need you to find them," the Wolf told her.

"I've some satellite images that I'll send you," Mrs. Josephine informed him. "They show Kobblestone's vehicle parked on the side of the road at the base of Stryker's Peak."

"I should've known he would get involved," he snarled as the photo of a green Cruiser appeared on his dashboard. He was able to zoom in and could see one of the children standing outside the truck. "When did you get this?"

"The image is time stamped twenty minutes ago."

"Of course it is," he smoldered. "I'm already behind."

"Don't worry," she told him, trying to smooth over the situation. "They're just children. You'll catch them and then recover the compass for the organization."

Mrs. Josephine was very talented when it came to managing the field agents. She had been with B&P as long as anyone could remember. The Black Wolf respected her and gave silent thanks that she was his handler for this mission. He swung the car around and cut through the median, tearing up the grass as he raced back towards Stryker's Peak.

CHAPTER NINE

The main room in the old building smelled musty with stale air. The beam from the flashlight shined off the particles of dust in the air, making a perfect cone of light. There was a green sofa sitting against the opposite wall. It was covered with dirt and cobwebs. The sofa was the only piece of furniture in the room and it had clearly seen better days. There was a door to the right that led to an office.

Wyll walked over to some stairs leading to the bottom floor of the building. Unfortunately the stairs had completely fallen apart from the years of neglect. The floor creaked with every footstep and the floor boards felt like they would give way at any minute. It made Wyll very nervous.

"What do you see?" Annora asked from the door way.

"Broken stairs," he told her. "It looks like we'll have to find another way down. I bet it's a storage area. It sounds like the perfect place for an old blue lantern if you ask me."

"Well, that doesn't help us then, does it? You find a way down to that room and I'll see what's in the office."

She pulled out her cell phone and used the light to see in the office. There was a large wooden desk with a leather chair behind it. In front of the desk were two chairs. A wooden cabinet stood across the room. She opened the window blinds, but a dark mine doesn't let in any light. Using her light, she searched through the cabinet and the desk's drawers but the lantern was nowhere to be seen.

Wyll was determined to get down into the bottom room. He considered walking on the edge of the stairs but noticed some pieces of wood were broken there as well.

As he was scanning the room with the Maglite he noticed the flooring beneath the sofa was a different shade of brown. He hurried over to the sofa and set the light down on a cushion. Grabbing the arm of the sofa, he slid it away from the wall to see if there was a secret door underneath, one that hopefully led down.

The floor shifted and shook with a loud cracking noise. Then the floor beneath the sofa began to creak and moan, then with a crash, the sofa went down into the lower room. Dust and wooden splinters flew into the air, showering Wyll. He was holding onto the arm of the sofa. As it fell down, it pulled him with it into the new hole in the floor.

He flipped over the arm and landed on the sofa, shooting an explosion of dust into the air. Annora came running into the room to see what had happened. Wyll was coughing terribly.

"Are you all right?" she asked him.

"I'm fine," he said with a wave of his arm. He grabbed the flashlight to look around the room. There were crates and old mining equipment everywhere. In the far corner of the room was a shelf with a couple of lanterns on it. He got up and walked over to see if one was blue.

"At least there's some good news," she called out to him.

"What's that?"

"You found another way down."

"Ha-ha!" he said. "I've got better news…I found the blue lantern!"

"Are you sure it's the one?"

"It's the only blue one."

He reappeared next to the sofa holding up a rusty old blue lantern. She smiled and then reached down to grab it. He handed her the lamp and then with her help he was able to get back up to the main level.

"Let's go find that compass," he said with renewed treasure hunting energy.

CHAPTER TEN

The Wolf pulled off the road close to the spot where the kids had entered the forest only twenty-five minutes earlier. He was fuming mad because they had a head start on him. The creatures and animals didn't make a sound when the Wolf entered the forest. He left the car parked on the side of the road.

"Is this the spot?" he asked Mrs. Josephine. In his ear was a small receiver to hear her with and around his neck was a whisper-net system. Whisper-net was a high tech communication system that allowed him to stay in constant communication with Mrs. Josephine.

"According to our satellite, you're just south of their exact location. The mines are one mile to your east."

The Wolf slung a messenger satchel over one shoulder and started the hike towards the mines. His idea of supplies was a little different than the stuff Wyll brought with him. In the satchel was a rope, a flashlight, and a gun.

The ground was dry now, the sun having come out since the kids passed through. He was able to jog at some points and it didn't take him nearly as long to get to the mines. He removed the boards as quickly and quietly as possible; not wanting to alert them that he was there. The element of surprise always seemed to work in his favor.

***

Kipling sat in Sandy's at the same table the kids were sitting at earlier in the day. He was enjoying a delicious reuben sandwich with a tall glass of ice cold root beer. The day was growing colder and the sun was preparing to set behind the trees.

An old man with white hair and a bushy white mustache entered the cafe unnoticed by most of the guests, but not by Sandy. She moved her head in the direction of back table and the old man tipped his brown hat in gratitude. Without asking for permission, he sat in the chair across from the young man. Kipling looked up at the old man and smiled.

"Thaddeus, what are you doing in town?"

"Just doing some recruiting."

"Oh, I knew that boy with Annora looked new to me. When did you recruit him?"

"Just yesterday."

After the last customer left the cafe, Sandy locked the front door. It was closing time and luckily she didn't have to raise suspicion with the town's people by asking them to leave. She grabbed something to eat from behind the counter and joined the two men at the back table.

"So, Thaddeus," Sandy said, sitting at the table. "What's new?"

"I need your help."

"With what?" Kipling asked him.

"This was supposed to be a routine recovery of a lost artifact. Unfortunately things have changed and the kids may be in danger."

"The Wolf?" she asked.

"Yes, as far as we know right now he just entered the woods and is heading towards the mines and that was a little while ago. By now he's probably already entered the mines and we fear for the kids safety. I'm not really worried so much about Annora but Wyll is new to all this and..."

"And you're wondering if I would go and get them?" Kipling cut in.

"Most definitely!"

"I told you I should've stayed with them in the first place," Kipling told Sandy.

"I thought we could throw the Wolf off their trail. I didn't know that he already knew where they were heading."

Kipling stood up, finishing the last bite of his sandwich and gulped down the last of his drink. He grabbed his coat and hat then started towards the back door. Within minutes everything had changed.

It was now a rescue mission.

CHAPTER ELEVEN

They had tried to light the lantern but there wasn't any oil in it, so they continued to use their light, hoping to find some oil further into the mines. The light was supposed to guide them to the treasure, but if they couldn't get it to light, it wasn't much good to them. The kids were already a great distance down the mine shaft leading away from the Cathedral Room when they heard a loud crashing sound. They both stopped and looked at one another, then back towards the mine's entrance.

"What do you think that was?" he asked her.

"I don't know, but I don't want to wait around to find out," she told him.

They started running down the tunnel and came to a T-shaped intersection. Wyll looked left and right then pulled out the map.

Annora shined the flashlight on the map and found the 'T' on the map. Next to it there was an arrow bending to the right.

"I guess that means we go to the right," Annora said, pointing to the arrow.

"Okay let's hurry and get here. It looks like it might be an elevator."

They were running down the tunnel when suddenly light flooded it. There was a light bulb every fifteen feet or so, connected by a long electrical cable and bolted right into the rock ceiling of the mine.

"We're definitely not alone," Annora said to Wyll.

"I bet it's the Wolf," he told her.

Their run turned into an all-out sprint and by the time they reached the elevator they were both out of breath. Annora leaned against the wall and Wyll bent over holding his knees.

In front of them was an old elevator with a cage for a door. On the right hand side of the door were six levers with a ball-shaped hand grip at the end of each. Just beneath each lever was a number in numerical order from one to six. They both tried to open the cage door but it wouldn't budge.

On the left hand side of the door was a large plaque with a lot of writing inscribed into it. The title across the top read, "The Battle of Brigand Hill, 1825 A.D." Wyll read the story and although the story was cool he didn't understand why it was there.

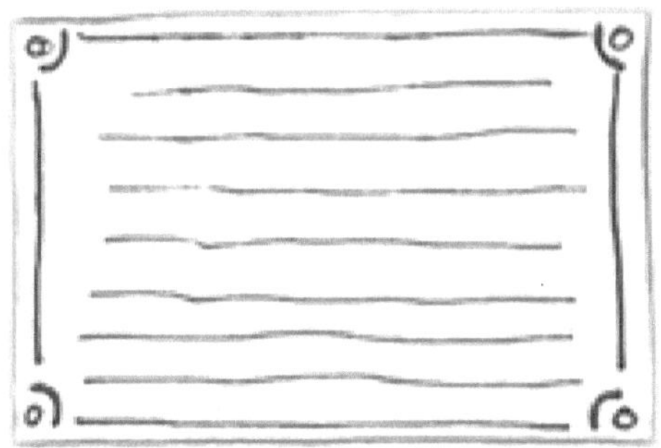

The Towne of Milton sat at the bottom of Brigand Hill, it was called this because there was a band of brigands which lived there and would come down to raid the towne. The captain of the guard, Filmore Stilton, decided to remove this problem and bring the fight to the brigands. Captain Stilton brought in soldiers from the surrounding towneships. In the morning he led five-hundred soldiers onto the field of battle. After a bloody start he lost two-hundred thirty eight. His men thought that all was lost until two-hundred commonfolk came from the Towne of Milton. The troops charged forward with a renewed energy and destroyed the brigands camp with a loss of only one-hundred men.

"The story has to be a clue," she told him, "otherwise, why would it be here?"

"Yeah, but what does it all mean?"

"What does it say?"

"It talks about the battle to regain Brigand Hill. It says how many people were there and what their losses were and then talks about reinforcements. Then it repeats the cycle of who they lost and who they gained and in the end they were victorious over the brigand clan."

"Well, we need to hurry up and figure it out or whoever is in the mine with us is going to catch up to us."

"The map!" he said pulling it out and looking at it again. "Yep, it makes perfect sense now."

"What does?"

"Soldiers will rise and soldiers will fall," he read from the map, "what matters the most are those left at the wall."

"What do you think that means?"

"It's a math equation," he told her. He read through the story again quickly. He started with the number of soldiers and subtracted the losses. Then he added the reinforcements and continued this until victory.

"Three hundred and sixty-two, that's the answer."

"Are you sure?"

"Of course, I am!"

"Good, hurry up then."

He slid the map back into his backpack then stood in front of the levers. He pulled the levers three, six, and two and a loud clicking noise sounded. The cage door sprang open and they pushed it the rest of the way. Annora glanced down the tunnel while entering the elevator and saw the Wolf running towards them. She jumped and pulled the cage closed, then looked at all the lit up buttons. All of them looked really old and worn except one at the bottom that looked pretty new. She pressed it quickly and the elevator started to move down. The top of the elevator disappeared beneath the floor just in time. The Wolf skidded to a halt in front of the cage.

"It's definitely the Wolf following us," she told Wyll.

"How do you know?"

"I saw him running down the tunnel while we were getting on the elevator."

It felt like it took forever before the elevator came to a stop at the bottom of the mine. The ride down was terrifying; it shook, rattled, groaned, and at some points it even felt like it was free-falling. Wyll jumped out, relieved to be alive and on solid ground. Right before Annora got off the elevator, she used the handle of her flashlight to smash the bottom button.

"Why did you do that?"

"So it resembles the other buttons," she told him. "Now he won't know what level we're on."

"Good thinking."

They walked deeper into the mountain.

CHAPTER TWELVE

As they walked further into the mines Annora listened for the motors of the elevator to turn on again, but either it never happened or they were too far away to hear it. Eventually they came to a large mine cart sitting in the middle of the tunnel on some tracks. Just next to the cart was a conveyer belt that ran upwards, disappearing into an opening in the rock. Wyll peeked into the cart, half expecting someone to jump out; but there was nobody in there.

"Do you think anyone could come down the conveyer belt?" he asked.

"Rule number one, Wyll: expect the unexpected," she said.

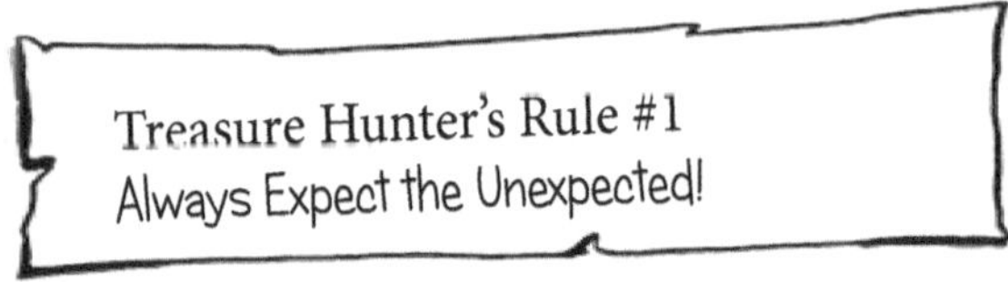

Just beyond the cart the mines took a significant drop downwards. The tracks ran down as far as they could see, then disappeared at the drop off. Annora nudged Wyll in the arm. When he looked over she had a strange smile on her face and a sparkle in her eyes.

"Don't even think of it," he said reading her mind.

"Come on," she pleaded, "I saw it in a movie once and it looked like so much fun."

"Those are called special effects and professional stuntmen."

"Where's your spirit of adventure?" she asked and then added, "Treasure Hunter."

He just shook his head in surrender and climbed into the mine cart. It was covered in dirt and crushed rock dust. She let out a gleeful, "Yes!" then climbed in with him after giving it a little push. There were loud squeaks and squeals with every turn of the wheel.

Eventually they faded away as the cart picked up momentum. Annora sat up higher to watch where they were going. The wind was racing through her hair.

"I guess this isn't so bad," Wyll called out to her.

"I told you so," she yelled back. And just then the cart took a quick left turn. It went up on two wheels and Wyll slid to the right smacking his head on the side of the cart. A bright light flashed in his eyes and he felt like he might pass out. He rubbed his hand against the already growing lump. When he looked up he saw Annora sitting back down holding onto the sides.

"I take that back," he told her. "This was a terrible idea and if we survive this I'll be shocked!"

She just smiled at him while swaying and bouncing with the movement of the cart. They were moving so fast now that the tunnel walls were nothing but a blur.

Wyll turned to looked ahead of them and saw an opening to the tunnel. The track just continued straight out from the tunnel and then disappeared through a large sheet of water falling down around the track.

"We are going to run right through the waterfalls!" he yelled pointing at the water.

"Hold on!" she yelled.

Their hearts raced, threatening to pound right through their chests as the falls came closer and closer. Wyll closed his eyes and said a quick prayer. He opened his eyes just as the cart slammed into the wall of water, bursting through and out the other side. Fortunately the cart remained on the track and all that happened was the bottom of the cart had filled with some water. His fear was now replaced with excitement.

"Now that was awesome!" he shouted.

Annora just sat there with a strange smile on her face. At that very moment, she knew that Thaddeus had made a good choice. During her time with the Adventurer's Guild, she had discovered that fearlessness was not always the greatest trait. A good adventurer, in her eyes, was cautious but willing to take a chance when need be.

The cart continued on down the track. Wyll looked down and immediately regretted doing so. They were over a hundred feet in the air on a wooden bridge. A large river ran through the mountain below them. Above them they could see another wooden bridge leading across the gap. It was not another cart track; it had hand rails for someone to hold onto when making the journey across. And the Wolf was doing just that, as he made his way across.

"There he is," Wyll said pointing up at the Wolf.

"We've got bigger problems," she told him pointing ahead of them. The track came to an abrupt halt on the other side of the gap. At the end of the track there was a large barrier with big metal studs sticking straight out. It was designed to stop a runaway cart.

"Do we have brakes?"

"NO!" she told him.

"This is going to hurt," he said and held tight onto the side.

The cart smashed into the barrier and flipped over it sideways. Both of them were thrown out of it. They landed on the ground rolling and sliding up against the cliff wall.

The ledge they were on was pretty big but unfortunately there was only one way off it. A metal ladder that was bolted into the cliff wall went straight up, but that was where the Wolf was. This ledge had another small waterfall coming down right onto one half of the ledge. The water ran across the ledge, making a short stream no more than fifteen feet long, and then it disappeared again over the lip of the ledge into the river below.

The rusty blue lantern had been thrown out of the cart in the crash. It was sitting in the stream jammed into a rock that stuck out of the water. Wyll let out a sigh of relief when he saw that it wasn't gone. They walked over to get it while trying to figure a way out. As he was picking the lantern up, the Wolf landed on his feet in the water right next to him. He had jumped down from the ledge above. Annora ran at him but he grabbed her by the face and shoved her backwards.

Wyll slipped and fell, still holding onto the lantern. He was quickly thrust forward by the force of the water, which sent him careening towards the edge of the ledge. He was holding onto the side handle of the lantern with one hand and using his other to try to stop himself.

"I will take that," the Wolf said as he grabbed the metal handle that ran across the top of the lantern. The Wolf tried to pull the lantern up while Wyll still hung on for dear life. He was suspended in midair by just the handle on the side of the lamp. Wyll looked up and then everything made perfect sense now.

Beneath its guiding light the treasure you will see.

The compass had been attached to the bottom of the lantern the whole time. Wyll reached up and grabbed onto the compass with his free hand. He twisted it and the compass came free. The Wolf saw it. He held onto the lantern with one hand and reached for the boy with the other.

"Give me the compass and I'll pull you up," he yelled to Wyll.

Wyll looked at the compass; it was like no compass he had ever seen. There weren't any hands showing the directions, just the markings on it for north, south, and so on. He looked at the Wolf and then at Annora, who was standing again. She realized what he was thinking and shook her head. The Wolf realized as well, but it was too late. Wyll had already let go of the lantern and dropped into the river below.

The Wolf stood there looking down over the side of the ravine. Then he shifted his gaze to Annora. She just shrugged her shoulders and followed her partner over the side. He couldn't believe his eyes. It was over a hundred feet to the river below and both kids just jumped down. He thought about it but changed his mind. The Wolf turned and went back the way he came. He'd find another way.

CHAPTER THIRTEEN

The water was freezing cold. The river raged through the mountain and dropped them both out the side of the peak down another waterfall. Wyll used every ounce of energy to hold onto the compass. After a hundred or so feet the turbulent water calmed down into a quick moving but somewhat smooth river.

Annora saw Wyll not too far from her and she swam up to him. He was so relieved and happy to see her that he could have kissed her. He raised his hand out of the water and showed her the compass.

"Awesome," she told him.

"Do you think the Wolf jumped in too?" he asked.

"No, I left him back on the ledge with his jaw on the ground."

"Really?"

"Yeah, you should have seen the look on his face when you let go."

They both had a good laugh. In the distance, they could see the large red brick bridge that led into town. It connected the road leading from the mountains to the road leading into town. The bridge looked majestic with the sun setting behind it. The bricks formed into arches that met in the middle. The water rushed around the center leg, choosing a path under the bridge.

"We can get out of the water by the bridge," Annora told him.

"Good," he said, "because I'm freezing cold."

They swam over to the side of the bridge and climbed out of the river onto the concrete walls. There were brick stairs leading up the side of the bridge to the street. The two of them just laid there on the ground for a while trying to catch their breaths.

Annora looked up the stairs and froze. Someone was standing up there next to an idling car. She couldn't make out who it was but she didn't want to find out either. As she helped Wyll to his feet she signaled him to be quiet and pointed up the stairs. The person began to turn around and would spot them for sure.

"Come on!" Annora said.

She and Wyll ran under the bridge across to the other side. The concrete retaining walls ended abruptly and the forest began. They were about to jump and make their getaway when they heard a familiar voice.

"Annora, Wyll, stop running," Sandy called from the top of the bridge. "It's me, Sandy."

They both stopped and looked up at her. The setting sun was now shining into her face and the kids could see her clearly. They almost fainted with relief. The kids crossed back over and climbed up to the car. Soon they were wrapped in wool blankets, sitting in the back of Sandy's jeep.

"So you recovered the compass?" she asked them.

"Yeah," Wyll told her. He pulled it out to get a closer look at it. The face of it had the eye etched into the front of it beneath the glass. The four letters representing north, east, south, and west remained but as Wyll had noted before, there were no hands to show the direction. He flipped it over and turned it around in his hands, looking at the gold casing with a gold rope decorating the edge. "I don't understand it. There aren't any hands to show which direction you're going in."

"We have to get it to the train station and drop it off with Thaddeus," Annora told her.

"I know," Sandy said. "I'm just waiting for our escort."

"Huh?" both kids said.

"Kipling went up to try and delay or stop the Wolf. He said that he would be right back." Almost on cue, a pair of headlights came into view coming down the mountain. Sandy turned the jeep around to face town, waiting for his cruiser to ride by them. As it passed by, she could see his shadow in the driver's seat. She followed behind him.

They pulled into the parking lot at the train station. She followed the cruiser in allowing Kipling to park first. As they started to pull in next to him Wyll noticed the passenger door opening. Sandy parked in the open spot on the driver's side of the Cruiser.

"Was anyone in the car with Kipling?" Wyll asked.

"No, it's just him," she told him. "Why?"

"I don't know for sure but I thought I saw somebody getting out of the passenger side."

"Stay here," Sandy told them and pulled a Taser gun out of the glove box. She slid out of her jeep and crept over to the Cruiser. She slowly and quietly made her way around both cars but there was nobody to be found. When she opened the door she saw that Kipling was tied to the steering wheel.

"Hi there," he said to her as she opened the door.

"What happened?"

"The Wolf happened," he told her, "I was trying to flatten his tires to delay him, when he got the jump on me."

She untied his hands. Kipling got out of the Cruiser to help her look for the Wolf. When they turned around to the back of the jeep he was standing there with the kids in front of him. He had a gun out and was pointing it at Sandy and Kipling.

"Don't try anything funny," the Wolf told them. "I just came for the compass."

"Well, you got it," Sandy said, "leave the kids alone and get out of here."

"I am, just drop that Taser you got there and I'll leave."

She tossed the Taser on the ground and it slid into the gravel by the front of the parking spots. The Wolf nodded in satisfaction and pushed the kids towards the two of them. He was just about to make his exit when there was a loud cracking sound and he stood up straight then fell to the ground in a heap. Standing behind him with a gnarly wooden cane in his hand was Thaddeus himself.

"Nobody threatens my treasure hunters," Thaddeus said with a smile. Kipling walked up and grabbed the compass from the unconscious Wolf's hand. Thaddeus pulled a black metal box out from the inside of his coat.

Wyll blinked in confusion, trying to figure out how he could have possibly fit that box in his coat.

He opened the box and Kipling dropped the compass inside of it. Thaddeus closed the lid and tucked it back into his jacket. He thanked the children and told them he would see them again. Kipling followed Thaddeus to the train and they both climbed on board. The train wasn't scheduled to leave until the morning but once Thaddeus was on the train it fired up and before Wyll knew it, the train was leaving the station. Sandy and the kids watched as it pulled away from them and disappeared into the darkness.

When they turned back around, the Wolf was gone.

CHAPTER FOURTEEN

The next morning Wyll woke up and got dressed, then joined his parents for some breakfast. His mom made Belgium waffles, his favorite. He piled fresh fruit and whipped cream on top of them.

"So did you have a good day yesterday?" his father asked.

"Where did you go?" his mother asked.

"I met a girl," he said, looking at his dad.

"Oh, very nice," his dad said, smiling at his son.

"And how did your clothes get wet?" his mother asked.

"I fell in the river," he blurted out before thinking.

"The river?"

"Ugh yeah, I was by the old red brick bridge."

"You were at Kissing Bridge with a girl you met?" his father asked with a little bit too much pride in his son. Wyll's cheeks flushed and he finished his breakfast quickly before being excused from the table. He didn't want any more questions, so he went into his father's office and stretched out on the couch. He turned on the lamp behind him and was going to read one of his comic books when he noticed a familiar book lying on the floor underneath one of the bookshelves.

He slid off the couch and crawled over to the shelf. On the floor was an old and worn out copy of the Treasure Hunter's Handbook. He pulled it out and flipped it open. Written on the inside cover was the name Wilhelm Tiberius Forthchild in blue ink. A look of wonder crossed his face.

"Dad?"

ALSO AVAILABLE FROM
TIM GOEHLE STUDIOS